Lots of circles,
round and round—
roll them,
bounce them,
all around!

Shake, shake, shake!

Shake the shapes—
what will they be?
Here's a **square**,
just for me!

Lots of squares,
all sides the same—
stack them,
join them,
play a game!

Shake, shake, shake!

Shake the shapes—
what will they be?
Here's a triangle,
just for me!

Lots of triangles,
points and sides—

tip
them,

tilt them.

They make slides!

Shake, shake, shake!

Shake the shapes—
what will they be?
Here's a **semicircle**,
just for me!

Lots of semicircles,
half circle style—
rock them,
wear them,
make me smile!

Shake, shake, shake!

Shake the shapes—
what will they be?
Here's a **rectangle**,
just for me!

Lots of rectangles,
standing tall—
build them,
climb them,
make a wall!

Semicircle!

Rectangle!

Now what can we do?

We can **ZOOOOO**

oom . . . across the room!

We can

soar . . .

Shake the shapes—
what will they be?
Here's a **circle**,
just for me!

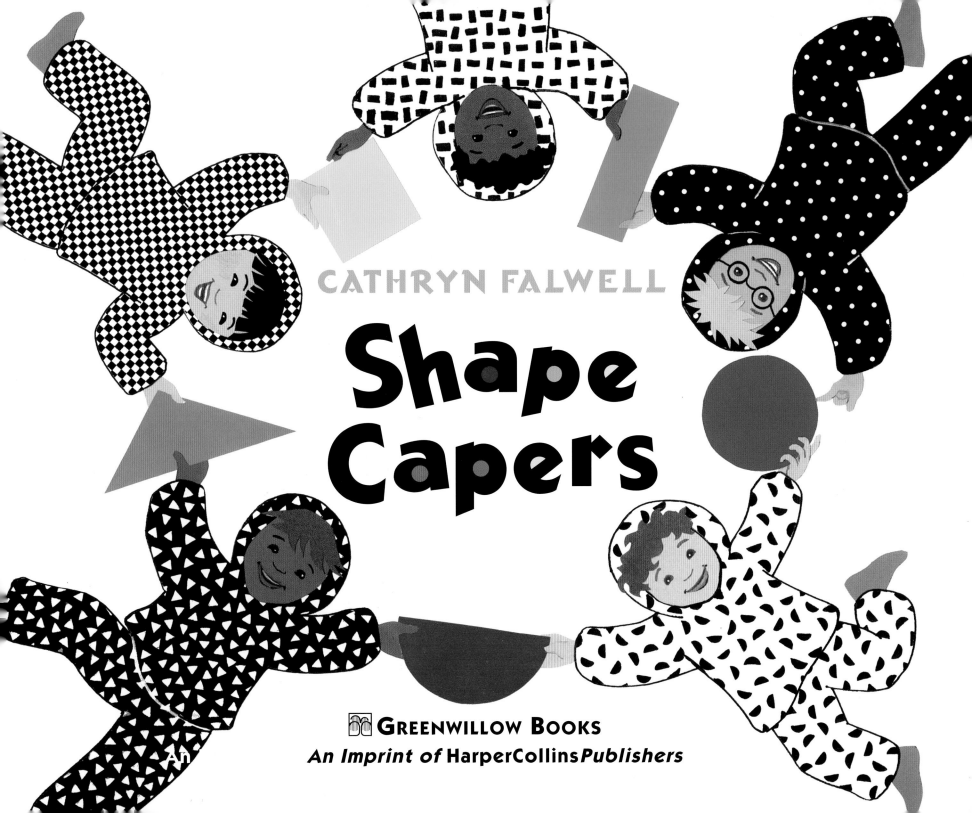

CATHRYN FALWELL

Shape Capers

GREENWILLOW BOOKS
An Imprint of HarperCollinsPublishers

Shape Capers
Copyright © 2007 by Cathryn Falwell
All rights reserved. Manufactured in China.
www.harpercollinschildrens.com

Cut paper, paint, and ink were used to prepare the full color art.
The text type is Kabel.

Library of Congress Cataloging-in-Publication Data
Falwell, Cathryn.
Shape capers / by Cathryn Falwell.
   p. cm.
"Greenwillow Books."
Summary: A group of children shakes shapes out of a box
and discovers the fun of using circles, squares, triangles,
semicircles, rectangles, and their imaginations.
ISBN-13: 978-0-06-123699-0 (trade bdg.)
ISBN-10: 0-06-123699-3 (trade bdg.)
ISBN-13: 978-0-06-123700-3 (lib. bdg.)
ISBN-10: 0-06-123700-0 (lib. bdg.)
[1. Shape—Fiction. 2. Imagination—Fiction.
3. Stories in rhyme.] I. Title.
PZ8.3.F2163 Sha 2007 [E] 22 2006043061

First Edition 10 9 8 7 6 5 4 3 2 1

Greenwillow Books

Shake, shake, shake!

For my family, with love

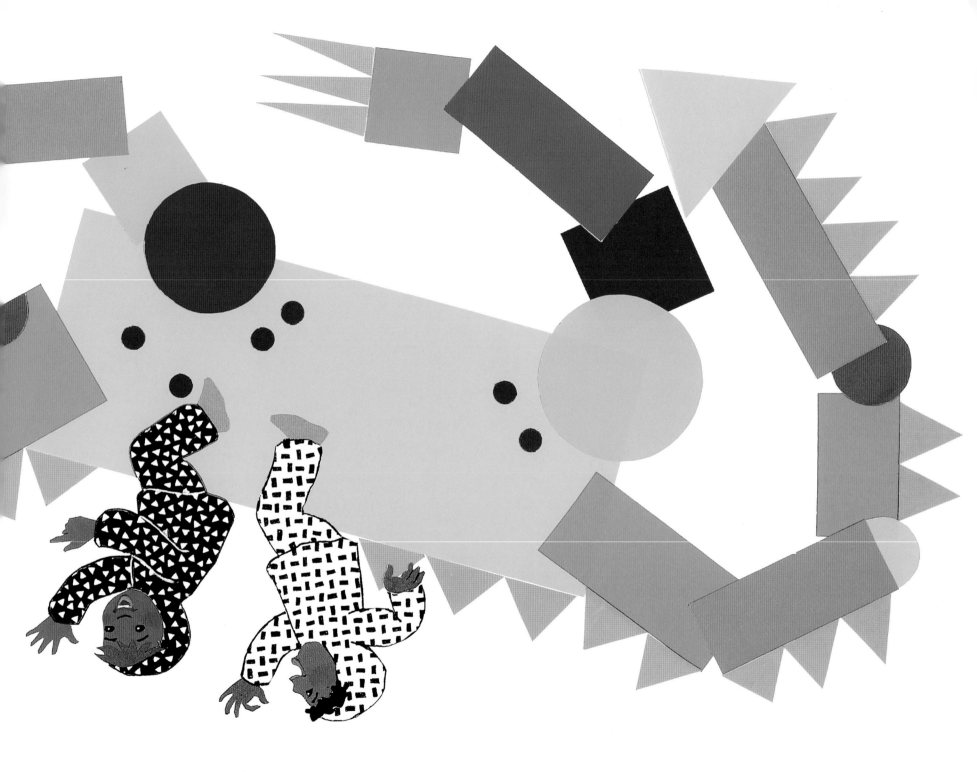

We can

ROAR!

We can play
with shapes all day!

"Hooray!"

Shapes are everywhere!

Where can YOU find shapes?

How many circles do you see?

How many squares can you find?

How about triangles, semicircles,

and rectangles?

You can make shape pictures!

Cut shapes from all kinds of paper:

old magazines and newspapers,

wrapping paper, greeting cards,

and other scraps.

Glue the shapes together!